This book is dedicated to all the men and women who are guardians of our forests.

Tales of the Old Moose

Written by

Benjamin Scribner

Illustrated by

Margaret Rose Scribner

TALES OF THE OLD MOOSE

Many years ago when I was a young boy of nine or so, my family moved to a small town in New Hampshire that nestled in the shadows of Moose Mountain. New to the neighborhood, I hadn't yet met any boys of my age so I spent many days by myself, exploring the woods around our home.

Back in the day, it was not unusual for young kids like me to go hiking in the woods all alone. Of course, I first had to tell my parents where I was going—though wandering aimlessly in the woods can make it hard to say where—and for how long I might be gone. The normal parental order was to be home before supper.

It was thus that I spent those early spring days: hiking along forest trails, wading in small streams, sometimes catching the occasional unwitting frog—to examine and then return safely to its home.

On one such warm, late spring morning I decided to trek farther into the woods than I ever had before, and climb higher up the mountainside than I had ever climbed before. It was there, on that mountain, where the strangest adventure of my young life began.

As I hiked deeper in and higher up the mountain, I began to think I might be a little bit lost, and I felt a little bit scared. Not scared of being lost—but of having to suffer the wrath of my mom for being late for supper!

I had just about decided to turn around, retrace my steps, and find my way home, when I spotted the oddest little house—seeming to grow right out of the forest floor—and sitting in the midst of a sundrenched clearing. However, to say it was a typical "house" would be far from the truth. This small abode emerged from a very large tree stump, rising skyward for some twenty feet or so. It was crowned by a steeply pitched roof, shingled with rough-cut shakes, and topped off with a crooked little chimney ... puffing smoke.

The front door was framed on both sides by a small window, and a large, rustic porch wrapped itself around it.

While I huddled there among the trees, basking in the morning sun, this extraordinary apparition made me wonder if I had crossed into some mystical time-warp. And ... as if all this wasn't weird enough, the largest rocking chair I have ever laid eyes on sat to one side of the door.

As I stood staring in amazement at this baffling spectacle, the door swung open and a very large and seemingly very old moose stepped out and immediately arranged his sizeable posterior into the rocking chair. His eyes glistened of ancient wisdom, appearing to reflect far back into another place and time—while seeming to gaze far into the future as well. His hide was a mottled gray, his antlers gnarled and bent, making them appear smaller than might be expected for so large a moose.

"Come here, young Benjamin," the moose said in a voice sounding like gravel tumbling along a stream bed. "I have been expecting you. Please. Come sit."

"You ... can ... talk?" I stammered, thinking maybe I should run home and never come into these woods again.

"Why, yes, of course I can," he said as he reached for a wooden mug full of something steaming pleasantly and handed to him by a bustling little gray squirrel. "I know your language. I know many languages—many tongues. Now please come join me here on this porch."

Well, I quickly decided being late for supper, and lost, was nothing compared to visiting a talking moose. So I moved toward the stone steps. I was only a few paces away when a rather roly-poly badger crawled out from beneath the porch and he commenced growling and pawing the ground in front of me! I jumped back, turned, and was about to run, when the old moose spoke again.

"Badger," he said in a scolding voice. "I have *invited* young Benjamin to sit with me. He is my guest—and now yours too. Behave yourself!"

The badger stopped, looked over his shoulder at the old moose, shook his head, kinda shrugged his shoulders, then turned on his heels, scrambled up the steps, and lay down.

"He wants you to sit next to him." the old moose said.

"He won't bite me?" I asked cautiously, tentatively placing my foot on the first step.

"Oh no, he's quite harmless. He's just putting on an act for you."

I sat down on the top step and the badger curled up in my lap, and almost immediately began to snore.

The old moose chuckled at this, and then asked, "Would you care for something to drink—ice tea perhaps?"

The same bustling little grey squirrel reappeared and set a wooden mug down in front of me that tinkled of ice chips. He chattered something incomprehensible to me, all the while making comical gestures with his front paws causing the old moose to chuckle.

"He really wants you to try it." He said pointing at the mug.

"Thank you," I said to the squirrel as I picked up the brimming mug and took a sip. Ohhh . . . it was delicious!

I settled down on the top step as the badger began to snore even louder, and the old moose began his tale.

"I'm not exactly sure when I came to be on this earth" he began, "but you humans were not here yet—not on this side of the world."

I looked at him with something like disbelief plastered all over my face.

"It's true; there was a time when humans simply did not exist here."

Now in my young mind humans had always been here—and always would be—but I had not studied ancient history yet, so this concept was quite a shock to me.

"I knew from my beginnings I was different from the others of my kind" he went on. "I could think, and learn new things, and contemplate on all those things I saw and heard."

He stopped to sip his tea. "Once I learned the languages of all the other creatures that shared this earth with me, then new—and strange—creatures began to make their appearance. They walked upright—on two legs. They appeared to have no language—none that I recognized—just strange guttural sounds with strange hand gestures that I could not understand."

"You mean us—people like me?" I asked, not so much as to interrupt him, but because I really wanted to understand more fully this tale he was relating to me.

"No," he explained, "Those first people you know as Native Americans. They came across a great land bridge from the other side of the world. Your people didn't arrive here until many years later."

"I watched them with some interest at first, slowly learning their ways." He stopped for another sip of tea. "I always stayed out of sight of course, because they hunted, killed, and ate many animals, and I didn't wish to become one of their meals."

Just then a perky little chipmunk made an appearance, ran up my pant leg and snuggled down in my lap next to the snoring badger as the moose continued on.

"I followed them as over time they made their way across this vast country establishing their dwellings and villages. It took many years for them to accomplish this, and as their habitat grew and prospered their means of communication developed also, but breaking off into many different dialects as they split off into many different tribes. I eventually learned them all." He stopped there. "It is getting late young Benjamin and you don't want to miss your supper. Come now, it is time to head home, we can talk as we walk." And with that he stepped off the porch and with him lumbering along beside me we headed down the mountain back to the trail from which I had so recently come.

The old moose chatted on. "Some time later I saw your people when they arrived. First in a place now known as Virginia, then later in the northern place called Massachusetts—just next to your beloved

New Hampshire." He continued on as we walked. "They were strange folk—not necessarily to my liking. You see, the Natives lived *with* the land, only taking what they needed, never wasting anything. These new people attempted to *tame* the land, to take from it—and not give back. They made the creatures and the resources of the land and sea do their bidding, not allowing the land or the sea to provide for them by the rules of nature. In time they soured the very soil and the seas their lives depended upon."

We walked on in silence for a time, and then he continued.

"Many of those newcomers died that first year, and that was sad. But sadder still were the horrible diseases they brought with them that the Natives knew nothing of and consequently many of the Natives died as well."

"Couldn't you have helped them?" I asked. I knew nothing about the diseases he spoke of but I couldn't imagine a time, and place when there were no doctors or hospitals.

"There was nothing I could do, as I knew nothing about the diseases they brought from the other side of the world. And——had I tried to help them they might have killed me before I'd had a chance to share my knowledge with them." He hung his head, remembering that long ago sad time.

"It is better to live with the land than against it" he added as though a benediction, just as we reached the final pathway to my home. It would be many years before I would understand that simple truth.

"Here you are young Benjamin—I will see you again tomorrow." And with that he turned and was gone.

"Wait! You haven't told me how you know my name!"

Too late. He was already out of sight.

I high-tailed it for home, all the while trying to decide if I should tell anyone about my strange adventure. Probably not—for they would never believe me.

The next morning Mom was amazed at how fast I dressed, brushed my teeth, ate my breakfast, and finished my morning chores. I rushed from the house yelling a promise over my shoulder that I would be back in time for supper.

When I arrived at the old moose's cabin, a big black mamma bear was nearby playing with her two cubs. Mamma stood tall and growled when I came into view, but a word from the old moose calmed her down and her cubs ran up to greet me.

As much as I wanted to play with them I had to know the answer to my question of last night—the question I had asked moose just as we parted. So again I asked him — "How do you know my name?"

"I know many things about you young Benjamin," he responded. "I have followed you and your family for many generations."

"What?

Why <u>me</u>—and why my family?"

"It was foretold to me many eons ago, by the wise old shaman of an ancient tribe that roamed the earth. He told me I would meet many along the way who could change the course of history, but only if I taught them early the ways of earth and all that live upon it. His people were the guardians of this land and its people, and practiced what your people now call 'conservation'."

He explained further, "There have been many others before you that I have guided along on their journey toward the right path, and now it is your turn. You are the next to lead others into a better world."

"But I'm just a kid, what can I do?"

"You will not always be thus. Do you know that your great-grandfather was an elder of the Passamaquoddy People who lived among the tall fragrant pines and icy, blue lakes in the territory you know now as Maine? I knew him well. In his language I was called a 'mus', and my little friend here", he said pointing to the squirrel, "was called a 'mihku', and those bears over there?—they were called 'muwins'. You see, you were born to fulfill a very important legacy. When you are grown, and have seen many things, and learned many ways, all that I teach you now, in this place, you will remember, use and share with others to lead them to their right pathways."

"Now, go have some fun and play with those little cubs." The old moose said, "Just be careful—they may be small but they can play pretty rough."

He wasn't lying. Soon I was covered with scratches and cuts all over my arms and legs, but having the time of my life! Before long mamma bear called them to her and they loped off into the forest, and I went to sit on the porch.

"Young Benjamin, every experience is a learning experience. What have you learned from the bear?" he asked as the squirrel offered me a brimming mug of ice tea.

"That bear cubs play hard." I laughed, "And the mamma wasn't too happy to see me at first."

"Yes that is true; mamma bears are very protective of their young." and he took a sip from his mug. "And you must always remember that away from here, you must never put yourself between a mother bear and her young—or ever try to play with one. Only here is it safe for you to do this."

A lesson I would never forget, as with the many lessons I would learn that spring and summer. I would meet many creatures, some friendly, and some only friendly while in the company of the old moose. He would always caution me to be careful away from his cabin.

That evening when I got home my Mom took one look at me and exclaimed,

"What ever have you been doing! You look like you've been attacked by a bear! Go get in the bathtub, and put on some clean clothes before supper!"

I couldn't help but laugh and Mom gave me one of her "Mom" looks and pointed to the bathroom.

My dreams that night were filled with bears and moose and playing in the forest. But just before I fell into deep sleep I sat bolt upright in bed and thought "That moose knows my name but he never told me his!"

~~~~~

The very next morning I was back at the moose's door with the intent of asking him his name, but before I could the old moose came out on the porch and informed me we were going on a trip far out to the great Northwest region of this vast county to examine a mountaintop forest in a place that would eventually be known as Idaho.

"But I need to be home by supper!" I exclaimed, thinking a trip far away from home would for sure upset my Mom. After all, she didn't even know about my moose friend!

The old moose just laughed," You will be home long before you are missed young Benjamin. I know how to travel through time and space."

Well this was an interesting concept for my young mind, and as I thought about all the possible ways there were to travel as the old moose beckoned me inside his cabin.

Once inside I was astounded at all I saw in there. There was his bed, though extremely large it was very low to the floor.

A table made from logs was next to it and chairs on either side—one large and one just my size. There was also a small wood-burning stove sitting in a corner and being tended by the badger, who just grunted when he saw me, then turned back to his work. Shelves overflowed with all manner of things. I saw a globe and a telescope, and more books then I had ever seen in one place, and all stacked haphazardly on shelves, filling every nook and cranny, and spilling over onto the floor. Chipmunks and squirrels scurried all about the place.

"Sit." The old moose said, as he motioned to the smaller chair.

Just as I sat a saucy little chipmunk ran up my pant leg and burrowed into my shirt pocket. I was treated once again to a warm mug of tea by the squirrel.

"We will arrive in the blink of an eye" the old moose said as he sat down and made himself comfortable. Before I could utter a reply or sip my tea the old moose suddenly stood up again and walked toward the door. "We are here." I had felt nothing, no movement, or any hint that we had gone anywhere, and when the door opened

I expected to see the same trees, the same porch and rocking chair, the same woodlands that I had seen just moments ago when we enter his cabin.

~~~~~

Instead I found myself staring at an ugly decimated landscape of what once had been a flourishing forest. All that remained were jagged tree stumps, and piles of small chopped off tree tops littering the forest floor. Towering over all were huge slash piles that bordered crude roads running through this dreadful place. This was nothing like the woodlands back home!

"Where are we?" I asked feeling a little uneasy and a lot sad looking at all these stumps.

"We are in the northwestern part of your great country," the old moose said looking piteously miserable. "You will live here someday and this horrible legacy will be in your backyard, and it will make your heart ache."

My heart was already aching.

"As time goes on humans have become more and more disrespectful of the earth and all its gifts and resources. The early humans—the Natives—used everything, wasting nothing." he said. "Your people now waste more than they use! They must think the supply is non-ending."

I could hear the sorrow in his voice as he continued.

"I understand the human need for shelter, but not the need to destroy an entire forest for the few trees they need, and leave the rest just to rot."

"Won't these rotting trees provide nourishment to help new ones grow?" I asked hopefully, looking at all those destroyed trees that had been left behind.

"Yes, but a living tree is more beneficial to the forest than a dead one. It provides shelter for many living things, and even cleans the very air we breathe."

In my young mind I could see woodland creatures, like large deer, bear and moose needing the trees for shelter from the rain and snow, while the smaller ones, like birds and squirrels, roosting among the lush and sheltering branches.

"Many years ago, when logging was a new flourishing industry; they harvested only enough trees to fill their needs, leaving the rest to flourish." He went on, "Now it's faster—and cheaper—for those who come into these forests to wreak havoc on our woodlands—the giant logging companies have grown greedy. They hack down every tree on the mountainside and after their slashing is done they leave behind all trees that don't meet their needs, to rot on the forest floor. This forest may never recover—and without your help young Benjamin it is a sure thing that it never will." I saw a tear slide down his craggy old nose.

"My help?" I thought? But before I could ask, another moose—a much younger one—stepped out from behind a small pile of downed trees. The old moose lifted his head as the younger one bowed to him and stepped forward. He then came right up to me, looked me fully in the face and sniffed my hair! Then he turned away and headed back from where he had came.

"He has your scent now." The old moose chuckled, "He will pass that on to his offspring so when you arrive here many years from now, they will know you and respect you."

"But how can you be so sure that I will live here?" I asked. "Will my Mom and Dad move here too?"

"As I told you on our first day, I know many things. You will move to this mountain many years from now—when you are a man. You will live alone but with many friends nearby. But first you have many worldly things to experience, and very important lessons to learn before that can happen. Remember this above all else," he stated, "Work hard. Do not waste. Take from the Earth only what you need. Leave as much as you can for future generations. This will be your joy—your happiness—your legacy—what you were born to do."

And having said that he turned and together we went back inside the door we had so recently exited, and as he promised I was home before supper with the chipmunk still in my pocket!

Those were his words so many years ago. They echo in my mind—and in my heart—as I sit now on a mountaintop in the great northwest state now known as Idaho—just as he said I would. Below me, and as far as I can see loggers have savaged and ransacked the land, obliterated much of the forest. Trees left behind litter the forest floor like billions of dead corpses -and why? Profit. The logging companies have become greedier still. I hear the words of the old moose echo through my being, so I go down to the slash piles and gather the sad discarded remains of this forest to use to heat my cabin. I take only what I need. I gather the bigger logs for my many building projects. Little by little I am cleaning up the waste they left as best I can.

And of my remaining time with the old moose? It was to be sadly limited. I spent many days with him during my ninth summer. We hiked the nearby woodland trails. Me, studying animal tracks and learning all he had to teach me about the world. Some days we traveled alone, but some days we had company, either mamma bear with her cubs, or badger, or other dwellers of the forest.

He eventually told me his name. It was Wiyukcan Hexaka (Wi-Yuk-can Hex-a-ka). That was a strange name. I couldn't even pronounce it, and when I asked what it meant and he told me that in good time it would be revealed to me.

Often the old moose would send a chipmunk or squirrel off to find a certain plant for me to study, teaching me to identify those I could safely eat and those I could not. He taught me how to survive in the woods should I become lost, whether it be summer or winter. I learned respect for all living things—from the smallest bug to the largest creature.

Soon summer turned to fall, and I had to return to school, so my time spent with the old moose was shortened to brief weekends.

Then one day near the end of fall, when the air carried a hint of snow, he was gone. There wasn't even a sign that he had ever been there—no cabin—no porch—no rocking chair—nothing. I rambled about the woods for many days looking for any sign, but found nothing. To say I was sad would be a huge understatement. My Mom grew worried about me, asking what was wrong when I came home day after day and went straight to my room—and cried.

~~~~~~

A few years later while researching in the school library for a geography project I was preparing I stumbled upon information about the Lakota Indian Tribe. It was as though a celestial hoof (or antler) had led me to it. I discovered the old moose's name that was given him by elders eons ago meant, "Wise Moose". How appropriate. Reading further I was in wonder and both awed and humbled by what I learned about the tribe from which he had sprung.

~~~~~~

"The Lakota Native was a true naturist—a lover of nature. He loved the earth and all things of the earth, the attachment growing with age. The old people came literally to love the soil and they sat or reclined on the ground with a feeling of being close to a mothering power. It was good for the skin to touch the earth and the old people liked to remove their moccasins and walk with bare feet on the sacred earth. Their tepees were built upon the earth and their altars were made of earth, and it was the final abiding place of all things that lived and grew. The soil was soothing, strengthening, cleansing and healing."

~~~~~

Like all little boys, I grew up. Like some boys, I joined the Navy and sailed off to far away lands. My travels broadened my world and I learned a great deal about many different cultures, and experienced many wonderful things about people different from my own.

Eventually I married, raised a family, left the Navy and became a long-haul truck driver. That opened my world even fuller to the sights, sounds and senses of this great country. As an adult I had pretty much forgotten about the old moose until one winter day . . . sitting in my rocking chair, on the porch of my snug little cabin, atop a mountain in the great Northwest—in a place called Idaho—I remembered. The old moose reached across time and space and touched my soul. I knew at that moment Wiyukcan Hexaka was still educating me.

Then it came to me—like a bolt of lightening! All winter long a young moose has been lurking about my cabin. She watches me. She watches as I feed the chipmunks. She watches as I scattered seeds and stale bread about for the birds. She watches while the snowshoe hare finds a safe haven under my cabin floor. She watches as her moose brethren reap the benefits of the trails I pack hard after a night's snow. She watches as I retrieve the sad remnants of what once were the proud, living trees of this mountain. I've attempted to approach her several times—murmuring softly to her—offering her apples. With each encounter she allows me a bit closer. In the nighttime—while I sleep—she grows bolder—investigating my entryway—exploring my porch. I see her tracks in the early morning. I call this moose 'she' but as young as she is I can't be sure if it is a female cow or a male bull. She is still very young—older than a calf—possibly a yearling. I'm now very sure that one day in the near future she will come close—look me fully in the face—sniff my hair—and speak to me.

And now Dear Reader, so many years have passed since that summer of my ninth year—and now, while I am in the fall of my life, I finally understand the lessons the old moose imparted upon me. And so for now my tale must pause, but as with all good tales that bear heeding—there will never be an ending.

Wiyukcan Hexaka is not done with me yet.

Benjamin Scribner: - a retired disabled Navy Veteran - lives atop a mountain in Idaho and daily views the destruction of the magnificent forests by greedy timber operations. Other books by Benjamin: *"My Life Above the Clouds ~ In the Footsteps of Henry David Thoreau" ~ and* soon to be released *"Escaping a Life of Quiet Desperation - Walking in the Footsteps of a Modern-Day Henry David Thoreau"*. Benjamin lives in St. Maries, Idaho

Margaret Rose Scribner - Ben's Mom - wrote and illustrated *"Hannah's Incredible Cow"* now available through Creatspace - Kindle and Amazon. She plans her next illustrated children's book *"The Incredible Adventures of the Spaceship 'ANYWHERE' "* to be released later this year. Margaret lives in Deland, Florida.

Made in the USA
Middletown, DE
19 December 2017